A BAN[A]

squonk

JULIA JARMAN

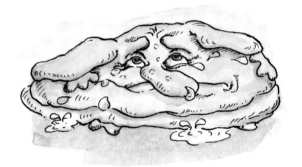

Illustrated by
JEAN BAYLIS

HEINEMANN · LONDON

The author would like to thank Bedford
Library and the Pennsylvania Bureau of
Travel Development for their help with
squonk research.

First published in Great Britain 1989
by Heinemann Young Books
an imprint of Reed Consumer Books Limited
Michelin House, 81 Fulham Road,
London SW3 6RB and Auckland, Melbourne,
Singapore and Toronto

Reprinted 1992, 1993
Text © 1989 Julia Jarman
Illustrations © 1989 Jean Baylis
ISBN 0 434 93062 8

A school pack of BANANAS 31-36 is
available from Heinemann Educational Books
ISBN 0 435 00105 1

A CIP catalogue record for this book is
available at the British Library

Printed in Italy by Olivotto

Chapter One

THE FIRST SIGN was a wet patch on the floor.

Sitting on the stairs, Jessica saw the wet patch – it was near her dad's case – but she was too miserable to take much notice. If the cat had done something – too bad. So far it was a Very Bad Saturday. Her dad had just come home from America. She had stayed in to welcome him – and he'd gone straight to bed! In the morning! And she could have gone ice-skating with Stacey.

The wet patch was spreading. She ought to tell someone. But everyone was sleeping, or cleaning. That was another thing, Granny Lewis – "Granny Loo-brush" Jessica called her – she was coming so it was a Mega-Cleaning day, a Really Terrible Saturday. She needed her dad. She needed him desperately, because Enormous Stanley Robinson was coming to get her.

Enormous Stanley said Jessica had stolen his best marble. She hadn't. The marble had rolled down the drain in the playground. But Stanley said he was going to tip her up, so that everyone could see her knickers, and shake her till the marble fell from her pocket. She had put jeans on, but she was still a bit scared.

It was no good asking her mum. Mrs

Dodd had said, 'Fight your own battles,
Jessica. Stand up to bullies.' Jessica
wanted to, but Enormous Stanley was
big and she was small for her age. Mrs
Dodd wouldn't say that to Charles
Edward Andrew Dodd – her Little
Prince. That's what she called Jessica's
brother. Jessica called him Pig-face.

Mrs Dodd was in the bathroom
bathing Pig-face, who looked more like
a pink pig than ever. He was squealing
too. Mrs Dodd was trying to wash his
hair.

'Mum,' said Jessica, 'there's a wet
patch . . .'

'Don't wanna . . .' wailed Pig-face
sending the shampoo flying. 'No Poo!'

Jessica closed the bathroom door.

4

Next she tried to tell Sandra Dodd.
Sandra was thirteen.

'Sandra, there's a wet patch . . .'

But Snotty Sandra was on the
bedroom floor, cucumber slices on her
face, head-phones over her ears.

Jessica picked up a towel.

She was on the bottom stair when the
wet patch splurged, and the cat who had
been sniffing the case, shot into the
kitchen.

'Badger, it's only a case . . . a
bottle . . . or something . . .'

'Swuff.'

A noise too!

'Swuff.' The case bulged slightly,
then went flat again.

It was very scary, but Jessica knelt
down, undid the buckles and lifted the
lid – and there it was!

A frog – that's what she thought. She
waited for it to jump.

Chapter Two

'QUIT STARING WILL ya.'

Jessica jumped.

The voice was American and croaky and quite loud.

'QUIT staring.'

She had to stare, she couldn't stop herself. She saw a wrinkled face with a long droopy nose – and droopy ears – and droopy eyelids. Behind the face was a body, also droopy, as if it were wearing a coat which was far too big for it.

'Where are your feet?'

No reply.

'I said . . .' She didn't finish. She had said the wrong thing. Tears flooded its eyes.

'Swuff. Swuff swuff swuff.'

'Don't,' said Jessica, 'please don't. You're making everything wet.'

And there was something else. Something much more serious.

Every time it sobbed it got smaller.

And the sobs were faster now.

Quickly but gently Jessica lifted it onto her hand.

'Don't cry, please. Tell me what's the matter.'

She stroked it – and it stopped crying, seemed to grow!

'You're supposed to be skeered,' it said at last. Skeered? Did that mean scared?

'I'm a squonk, from Pennsylvania,
I'm a he and – I – wanna – go –
ho . . o . . o . . me!'

Now the tears streamed down.

'What's a squonk?' The rest made
sense. Pennsylvania was where her dad
had been.

'I'm a squonk.' He seemed irritated
and the tears stopped.

Suddenly he grew – to the size of an
orange – and took a deep breath.

'I'm a FEARSOME CRITTUR!'

A fearsome creature? Jessica laughed and immediately wished she hadn't. He shrank again.

She spoke quickly.

'You frightened Badger.'

He stopped shrinking.

'And you frightened me – at first.'

'Did I?'

'Yes.'

He grew a bit.

'I have to be fearsome you see, in the forest, and I AM.'

He grew a bit more.

'I skeer skunks and possums and chipmunks and woodchucks and BLACK BEARS!'

He grew a bit more.

'I skeer raccoons and bobcats and porcupines and foxes – and LUMBERJACKS!'

He stood beside her now.

'But only sometimes.' His eyes filled up. 'And sometimes . . . swuff . . . they skeer me . . e . . e!' He collapsed like a punctured balloon.

Jessica picked him up.

It was very sad. Some of his relations had dissolved completely, he said. Poor thing.

'How did you . . .' she was just going to say, 'get into my dad's case?' when Mrs Dodd appeared.

'JESSICA!'

Squish! The squonk vanished.

Chapter Three

'WHY DIDN'T YOU tell me about this?' screamed Mrs Dodd, delving into the wet things.

'I did,' said Jessica looking at the bubbles in her hand.

'Must be this,' she said, holding up a bottle of shampoo.

Jessica started to search the hall.

Mrs Dodd scooped up the wet clothes and headed for the kitchen.

'Washing!' she shrieked, 'As if I haven't got enough to do.'

Jessica was frantic.

Where was the squonk? Help! He could be in the clothes.

She raced after her, 'Mum don't. Mummy wait.'

But Mrs Dodd was already piling clothes into the washing machine.

Clunk, went the door as she slammed it shut.

Now she was pouring in washing powder. Now she was twirling the dials.

Water gurgled through the pipes.

'Mummy! Stop!'

The door bell rang.

Mrs Dodd raced for the door.

In the washer the water was rising, and bobbing up and down was the terrified face of the squonk.

Clonk. She clunked a red knob – and the water stopped running in. Now for the door. Click. Nothing happened. Of course. If the door did open, water would rush out. Oh dear. What could she do?

Mrs Dodd came back.

'Mum, I'm sorry but there's something in the washer.'

'What sort of something?' said Mrs Dodd.

'A . . er . . something,' said Jessica, 'a present from Dad I think.'

Mrs Dodd frowned and then turned a knob. As the water level fell Jessica prayed that the squonk wasn't being pumped out with the water. Her mum opened the door. Jessica reached in and found the squonk. He was tiny and very, very still.

'Let's have a look then.'

But Jessica had gone.

She ran down the garden, cradling the squonk in her hands and talking softly. But it didn't grow, or shrink, or croak. It did nothing at all.

It was a Very Bad Saturday after all.

Chapter Four

SHE WAS JUST thinking that things could not possibly be worse, when they were!

For there was Enormous Stanley loping towards her! Like an American footballer with shoulders like tables, he had a horrible expression on his face, as if she were the ball, and he was going to throw her.

Help! Mum! Dad! No sound came out of her mouth.

Go away! No sound.

He was getting closer and closer.

She couldn't move.

His eyes bulged and his teeth were like a bulldog's.

'I want my marble, Jessica Midget Dodd. And I want it n . . .'

But he didn't finish. He had stopped, his mouth open. He was staring at something behind her.

What?

What had scared Enormous Stanley?

His face crumpled.

What was it?

Jessica turned and there behind her, two metres high, was the squonk, the *enormous squonk*. She had forgotten about him.

'SKIDADDLE!' said the squonk.

'Help!' cried Stanley.

When Jessica looked, he was hurdling
the side gate. Seconds later the front
gate banged shut.

That left Jessica and the squonk. He
was the same size as her now. She gave
him a big hug.

From then on it was A Very Good
Saturday. The squonk liked fir-trees,
the bathroom, especially the shower,
and English food.

Dinner was scampi and chips. Jessica

was secretly feeding the squonk, who was under the table, when Mr Dodd said something. Unfortunately the squonk had hold of her thumb at the time. He thought it was a chip.

'Little sister, Dad's speaking to you.' Snotty Sandra had a specially nasty way of saying 'little'.

The squonk let go.

'Sorry, Dad,' said Jessica.

'I was asking what you thought of the present?' said Mr Dodd.

'Great Dad. Really great. Thanks.' She hoped he wouldn't ask to see it.

'I got perfume,' simpered Sandra, 'What did you get?'

'A squonk,' said Jessica,

'Oh, a toy,' said Sandra – 'how nice.'

She didn't mean it, you could tell, and Jessica couldn't tell her that the squonk wasn't a toy, because he didn't want

anyone else to know.

'Toys – for the tinies,' Sandra continued, 'Look, Charles loves his.'

'Rrrrrr. Rrrrrr,' said Pig-face. He had a lumberjack set and was sawing through some chips.

Jessica was just thinking how she'd like to pull her sister's hair when Sandra's plate tipped up. Scampi, peas, chips and tartare sauce rolled down her sequined top and over her clean white trousers.

Sandra screamed.

Mrs Dodd rushed out.

Glancing down, Jessica saw the squonk stuffing himself. Then Mrs Dodd appeared with a brush and he sprang onto Jessica's knee.

Then the phone rang.

Jessica had to answer it. The squonk disappeared.

It was Granny Loo-brush. 'I'm on my way,' she cackled, 'Get the red carpet out.' It was her idea of a joke.

Chapter Five

DINNER WAS FINISHED in record time.
Then Granny Loo-brush arrived,
strutting up the path in a green trouser
suit, looking like a gigantic stick insect.

Mrs Dodd was opening the door – and
Granny was moaning already.

'Really, Veronica. Look at your hair.
And what have you got on? You look
like a scarecrow. Now if I can look
elegant at my age, I'm sure you can.'

Elegant! Her hair looked like a cauliflower, stiff and whitish yellow.

'And how's Jessica Mavis then?' Jessica HATED her second name. 'How about a kiss for your Grandma?'

Right now she was kissing Pig-Face. Poor Pig-Face, squirming to be free. It was horrible kissing her, like being hugged by a boa-constrictor.

Yuk – her turn now.

'And what have you got to tell me then, Jessica?'

Jessica knew what she was supposed to say. 'I got the main part in the school play and I came first in everything.' And then Granny would give her 10p.

Life wasn't like that, not for Jessica.

Her brain froze.

So there she was with her head bent backwards looking up Granny Loo-brush's nostrils, when an amazing

thing happened. The cauliflower hair moved, all of it.

And then, there it was, hanging from the lampshade – above it a droopy paw.

And there was Granny Loo-brush galloping through the hall door, her hands over her head.

Jessica and her mum couldn't stop laughing.

'You're terrific,' said Jessica to the squonk later.

Chapter Six

THE NEXT DAY was hard work. The
squonk was droopy and homesick. He
was pining for pine trees, the enormous
ones in Pennsylvania.

'Do you really want to go home?'
Jessica said at bedtime. She had made
him a bed at the bottom of her
wardrobe.

'Yea-swuff,' said the squonk.

'But what about me?' said Jessica.

'You'll make out,' said the squonk,
'You're bigger now, and you won't
shrink.'

She stood against her measuring
chart. It was true. She was bigger.

'And brainier and braver,' said the
squonk. 'I bet you could fix Enormous
Stanley now.'

'I'll talk to my dad,' she said. 'Perhaps
he'll be going back to America.'

The next thing she heard were little
squonky snores.

Chapter Seven

ON MONDAY THE squonk decided to walk to school with her. Cat-sized, he raced along, hiding, then springing from hedges and garden walls. But when she met Emma and Stacey he stayed hidden. They were talking about ice-skating, trying to make Jessica feel left out.

'Saturday was really great,' said Emma as soon as they met.

But Jessica was thinking about her promise to the squonk. She would miss him – and worry. He had had one very narrow escape. That's how he'd got here. Fleeing from some lumberjacks,

he had come to the edge of the forest,
seen a building – it was a hotel – dived
through a window and onto a bed.
Seconds later her dad had come in,
picked up the squonk and put it in his
case. He thought it was a free gift, a
Present from Pennsylvania. Poor
squonk . . .

'WELL?'

Jessica suddenly realised Emma was
talking to her. 'I said what have you
brought for it?'

'For what?'

'The project on America, stupid.'

Jessica remembered. They were going
to start a project on America today, and
everyone had to bring something
American to talk about. Emma and
Stacey were carrying plastic bags stuffed
full. An enormous glove was sticking
out of Stacey's.

'It's a baseball glove, and I've brought a ball, and my Snoopy sweat-shirt.' Her mum worked at the American air-base.

Emma had a collection of Macdonald's boxes, a cowboy hat, and the label off a tin of sweet-corn.

Stacey was comforting and said tomorrow would do. But Emma was determined to make her feel guilty.

'Oh Jessica, you told everyone about your dad going to America.'

'I'll bring something tomorrow,' said Jessica.

Chapter Eight

'AMERICA,' SAID MISS ANSTEE as soon as she had called the register. She wrote it on the board. She also wrote 'USA'.

'Now who can tell me what that means?'

'Nobody say nothing,' hissed Enormous Stanley from behind Jessica, 'or they get it, at break.'

'United States of America,' said Timothy Hunt who was a bit deaf.

'Very nice, Timothy, very nice indeed. Now who can tell me the name of a state in America?'

Suddenly Jessica felt brave and brainy, 'Pennsylvania, Miss.'

'Very nice,' said Miss Anstee, who didn't hear Enormous Stanley say, 'I warned you, Dodd.' And she didn't see his enormous leg reach out to kick

Jessica. Nor did she see him pull it back very suddenly, as if it had been bitten.

'And what do we get from Pennsylvania, anyone?'

'Vampires, Miss,' said Sophie Wickens.

Miss Anstee laughed and so did the rest of 4L, drowning a yelp from Enormous Stanley.

'No, no, that's Transylvania, Sophie,' said Miss Anstee, 'but it was a very nice try. Now, any more ideas?'

'Squonks,' said Jessica. And when even Miss Anstee looked doubtful she said, 'The squonk is a timid beast that lives in the hemlock forests of Pennsylvania. It has loose warty skin and when it cries it shrinks . . .'

As she talked, Enormous Stanley was taking the refill out of his biro. And while Miss Anstee was saying, 'I really

think we should look this up, 4L,'
Stanley was putting something into the
biro tube.

Then he raised it to his mouth.

'Ouch!' Timothy Hunt clutched his
head as rice grains shrapped the air.

'It was Stanley, Miss.'

Miss Anstee looked at Stanley who
had his arms folded and a 'Not Me,
Miss' expression on his face.

Was she going to be fooled? She
didn't look cross. She was staring at
something under his chair – a puddle.

'Oh dear, Stanley,' she murmured and walked up to him.

4L stared as she leaned over and put her arm around him. Next thing, Stanley with a very red face – and some very wet trousers – was walking out of the classroom.

Miss Anstee followed him.

'Stanley Robinson's Got Wet Pants On,' yelled Sophie Wickens. 4L cheered and banged on their desks.

'Okay cool it!' It was the squonk, sitting at Miss Anstee's desk. You should have seen 4L's faces.

Chapter Nine

'THANKS, SQUONK,' SAID Jessica, when they were walking home – he was in her school bag, 'Thanks for everything. I'll talk to my dad tonight.'

She had to – it was only fair.

So when Mr Dodd came upstairs to kiss her goodnight, she told him – and he laughed.

'It's true, Dad.'

He still laughed.

'Dad, it's TRUE.'

'That's enough, Jess. Goodnight.' He put out the light and ran downstairs.

'He's in the wardrobe!' she yelled after him, but he didn't come back to look. When she opened the wardrobe the squonk was asleep, but his pillow was wet and he was smaller than the hot water bottle.

Tuesday was a 'Very Bad Word The Alarm Hasn't Gone Off' morning. It was too late to walk to school. Mr Dodd had an important meeting at ten but said he could take the girls if they were quick. First they dropped Sandra at Brookfield Upper. Then they headed for the Middle School. It was already nearly nine.

'Don't worry, Jess, I'll take the short cut.'

That was all right until steam puffed out of the engine. Mr Dodd braked to a halt.

'Out, Jess!'

Out they jumped as turquoise liquid gushed into the gutter.

'Blast!' said Mr Dodd. When the spluttering stopped he lifted the bonnet. A pipe had come loose. He got a screwdriver from the boot.

'That's fixed that,' he said after a minute, 'but we need water. Fast. The radiator's empty.' He looked at his watch again. It was a very important meeting he said. He just couldn't be late. They looked around. There were no streams or ponds and the nearest house was a mile away.

'You can have the orange juice from my packed lunch,' said Jessica.

'Thanks love, but we need more than that. It's no good, we'll have to fetch some.' He slammed down the bonnet and the horn honked.

And there was the squonk sitting in the driving seat.

'What the . . .?'

'It's the squonk, Dad, the one I told you about.'

Man-sized, he was banging on the window now. Mr Dodd seemed paralysed.

'Let him out, Dad.'

Mr Dodd opened the door.

'Pleased to meet you, sir,' said the squonk. 'Water, did you say?' His big brown eyes filled with tears. 'Where do you want it?'

Mr Dodd lifted the bonnet.

Five minutes later they were speeding along the road.

That did it. A week later Jessica was waving goodbye to her dad and the squonk as they boarded a plane to America. (The squonk was in Mr Dodd's coat pocket.)

'Goodbye, Squonk!' Jessica felt sad, but happy too. She would miss him, but she was doing the right thing. If he was brave enough to take his chance alone then so was she. She was bigger and braver and brainier now. She was looking forward to Monday anyway – she had this great trick to play on Enormous Stanley!

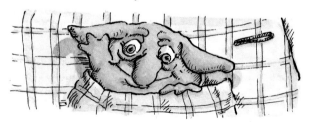